HOW DOES IT FEEL TO BE *OLD*?

HOW DOES IT FEEL TO BE *OLD*?

by Norma Farber

illustrated by Trina Schart Hyman

A Unicorn Book

E. P. DUTTON   NEW YORK

Library of Congress Cataloging in Publication Data

Farber, Norma.　　How does it feel to be old?
(A Unicorn book)
SUMMARY: Old age explains to youth some of
the thoughts and feelings, advantages and
disadvantages that accompany being old.
1. Old age—Juvenile literature.　[1. Old age]
I. Hyman, Trina Schart.　II. Title.
HQ1061.F37　1979　301.43'5　79-11516　ISBN: 0-525-32414-3

Published in the United States by E. P. Dutton, a Division
of Elsevier-Dutton Publishing Company, Inc., New York

Published simultaneously in Canada by Clarke,
Irwin & Company Limited, Toronto and Vancouver

Editor: Emilie McLeod　　Designer: Riki Levinson

Printed in the U.S.A.　First Edition　10 9 8 7 6 5 4 3 2 1

to Emilie, who asked the question
and Trina, who helped answer it

How does it feel to be *old*?

Very nice.
I don't have to listen to parents' advice
Such as "Watch where you step!" "Don't slip on the ice!"
"Come in from the cold!"
"Take off your rubbers!" "Now tie your shoe!"
Nobody's telling me what to do.
If somebody does, I just don't hear.
Do I make myself clear?
I please myself, make my own choice.
(Sometimes I miss my mother's voice
and my father's way—so tall, so grand—
of taking me firmly by the hand.)
Nobody's telling me. (All the same
I'd like to be called by my childhood name.)

How does it feel to be *old*?

Quite brave, quite bold!
I say what I choose—
having nothing to lose
by being a demon, taking a chance.
No punishment.
I can afford
to be mean, cranky and mean,
ranting and raving.
I've nothing to get—
no kiss, no reward—
for proper behaving.
I come, I go,
as though—as though
nobody cared if I came or went.
I'll scream if I will.
And still,
and yet,
nobody's made me cry in years.
(I miss the hug coming after the tears.)

How does it feel to be *old*?

Free, free, free!
I'm living alone and I eat
as much as I'm able.
One meal a day, or a couple, or three,
whenever I wish, and snacks in between,
all day, all night,
or never. Fat or lean,
no fuss about losing
my old, old, old, old appetite.
Do I feel like a treat?
I *take* it! (A waste,
sometimes—it hasn't the taste
that it used to. . . .) Oh well.
No fuss. So free! . . .

No excusing
myself from the table.
Oh wonderful way to be,
so quite by myself and me.
(Well,
when are you coming again to tea?)

How does it feel to be *old*?

Agreeable!
Your parents scold
if you stay up late.
Come spend the night; we'll talk till we fall
asleep in the midst of a game of cards.
If you drop a plate
at breakfast—oh sorry, I *jump* at noises!—
I'll simply serve
you another. My dear, what a beautiful cuRve
ball
you throw! Now here's a new word for you: *shards*.
You say it. Speak up!
Why do you speak in a far-off voice?
You're making me hold my ear like a cup.
Shards! I'll phone the glazier as soon as you're gone.
(I wish your visit went on and on and on . . .
into the unforeseeable
future. What's *that*? What I haven't the faintest notion of!
Except, dear child, it's filled with my love.)

How does it feel to be *old*?

Clever!
If clumsy. . . .
Have you noticed how crayons *wobble* now?
And move so slow?
When your mother was little she called me *Mumsy*.
I'd draw her a house—she didn't know how.
And a kind of a horse.
Some bug or other.
Wings in a nest.
Now she calls me *Mother*!
She wishes (but doesn't quite say it) I'd rest.
What for? I'm always fresh and ready
for games whenever
you are (well, sometimes I get in a muddle).
Let's play! I don't mind losing at tic-tac-toe.
I'll follow the leader—that's *you*, of course.
I mind being rather unsteady
at leapfrog now.
But I *used* to beat you at jumping a puddle!

How does it feel to be *old*?

Come see.
Let's look in the mirror together.
Yes, yes! You begin
to resemble this old grandmother—
you do! Or will very soon.
Something about that stubborn chin
of yours. Look hard. Look again.
Oh not this wrinkled prune
that I am! Who I was back *then*!
The way I saw myself in the mirror,
a child like you.
My stubborn jaw!

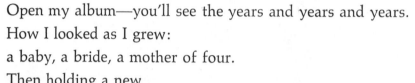

Open my album—you'll see the years and years and years.
How I looked as I grew:
a baby, a bride, a mother of four.
Then holding a new
granddaughter. There's more
to an old, old woman than what appears.
There's all that she's been before.
Before and after, both.
Well, who
am I being right now, exactly? The mirror's blurred.
Will you rub it true?
Here's a chamois cloth.

And here's this ring; just put it away
till it fits. There'll come a day.
Let's empty this drawer.
This watch needs fixing; it runs quite slow,
like me. I wore it a while ago.
I won't be needing it anymore.
I forget how it feels to be needing to be
in a certain *there* at a certain *then*.
I forget how it felt—for that was when
children, chores, oh how they all needed me!

How does it feel to be *old*?

Amazing!
The sun once again is blazing
and setting the sky
on fire. Sun's up! Well, so am I—
(don't rush me, please)
in a second, a minute.
This bed's so soft, I'd love to stay in it
an hour or two. I'm tempted to sleep
another three hours or four. . . .
Warm sheets—I feel like a lamb
in his fleecy sheepskin puff.
I'm dreaming the past
as though it never was over.
The pictures last and last and last. . . .
Digging for clams. Sinking sand.
Barefoot on beaches. Tanned
to a crisp. One perfect shell.
Picking on Strawberry Hill.
Flavor! Smell!
A country station. The train
coming in . . . going off. . . .
To be a child again. . . .
So warm, so deep,
under cover. . . .

Old woman, enough!
Get up! It's late!
I will! But you'll have to wait
till I stretch these old, old, old, old knees—
I'm getting there, really I am.
One foot at a time I'm touching the floor.
Soon I'll be standing—
but not too fast
or I might fall down.
I might disgrace
this old, old self by landing—
silly old clown—
flat on my face.
I'm up at last!
Like sun! You see?
I'm up! (And only barely recalling
the youngster who long, long ago was me
with never a hint of a fear of falling.)

How does it feel to be *old*?

In a rush!
So much to be done, so few
more years in which to do.
It's hard to remember I once had all
the time in the world to go up and down
and around the world,
travel to places great and small,
continents near and countries far,
China and Chinatown,
Arctic tundra, Australian bush,
the Amazon and Zanzibar.
If I were five or even ten,
I could live my life all over again.
But I'm not and I can't and I'm going to just
live out the rest that there is as I must.

How does it feel to be *old*?

Quite late.
There's somewhere I'm getting to, soon.
I haven't been told.
Not school. Not a playground. Nor house of a friend.
Not the moon.
Wherever it is, I'll open a gate. . . .
I'll be coming at last to an end—
or a start—I'm not quite clear.
I'll end what I've loved to be doing on earth—
my life right here—
since the day I was slapped on my bottom at birth.
I'll finish my *now* and my *here*.
(Remember the stories I told you, my dear.)
And nothing surprising
need come of the fact.

Have you noticed, I'm shorter, almost, than you?
I'm shrinking, you're stretching. What else is new?
Well, sun keeps rising,
journeys of planets continue exact.
Wind keeps blowing,
sky stays wide.
Soon you'll be knowing
that Grandma has died
while you are still growing
in inches and pride.